THE LOUD HOUSE

WINTER SPECIAL

PAPERCUTZ
New York

WINTER SPECIAL

nickelodeon  WINTER SPECIAL

"HUNG WITH CARE"
Kacey Huang — Writer
Kelsey Wooley — Artist, Colorist
Wilson Ramos Jr. — Letterer

"BARNYARD BLIZZARD"
Kiernan Sjursen-Lien — Writer
Way Singleton — Artist, Colorist
Wilson Ramos Jr. — Letterer

"COCOA LOCO"
Kristen G. Smith — Writer
Zazo Aguiar — Artist, Colorist
Wilson Ramos Jr. — Letterer

"A GLITTERING RECIPE"
Julia Rothenbuhler-Garcia — Writer
Tyler Koberstein — Artist, Colorist
Wilson Ramos Jr. — Letterer

"PUPPET PUNISHMENT"
Kiernan Sjursen-Lien — Writer
Erin Hunting — Artist, Colorist
Wilson Ramos Jr. — Letterer

"FREEZE FRAY"
Kiernan Sjursen-Lien — Writer
George Holguin — Artist, Colorist
Wilson Ramos Jr. — Letterer

"SLEDDING THE GNAR"
Kristen G. Smith — Writer
Ron Bradley — Artist, Colorist
Wilson Ramos Jr. — Letterer

"MITTEN MAYHEM"
Kiernan Sjursen-Lien — Writer
Angela Zhang — Artist
Maaike Scherff — Colorist
Wilson Ramos Jr. — Letterer

"I, LILY"
Caitlin Fein — Writer
Daniela Rodriguez — Artist, Colorist
Wilson Ramos Jr. — Letterer

"MEOWY CATMAS"
Caitlin Fein — Writer
Kelsey Wooley — Artist, Colorist
Wilson Ramos Jr. — Letterer

"BEST IN SNOW"
Kiernan Sjursen-Lien — Writer
Daniela Rodriguez — Artist, Colorist
Wilson Ramos Jr. — Letterer

"OPERATION X-MAS"
Jair Holguin — Writer
George Holguin — Artist, Colorist
Wilson Ramos Jr. — Letterer

"GEO'S NEW HOME"
Kacey Huang — Writer
Kelsey Wooley — Artist, Colorist
Wilson Ramos Jr. — Letterer

"UNLIKELY SUPERHEROES"
Kiernan Sjursen-Lien — Writer
Zazo Aguiar — Artist, Colorist
Wilson Ramos Jr. — Letterer

"OCEANS 11" FROM THE LOUD HOUSE #11 "WHO'S THE LOUDEST?"
Derek Fridolfs — Writer
Tyler Koberstein — Artist, Colorist
Wilson Ramos Jr. — Letterer

ZAZO AGUIAR — Cover Artist
JORDAN ROSATO — Endpapers
JAMES SALERNO — Sr. Art Director/Nickelodeon
JAYJAY JACKSON — Design
ASHLEY KLIMENT, DANA CLUVERIUS, MOLLIE FREILICH, NEIL WADE, KEVIN SULLIVAN — Special Thanks
JEFF WHITMAN — Editor
JOAN HILTY — Editor/Nickelodeon
JIM SALICRUP
Editor-in-Chief

ISBN: 978-1-5458-0687-6 paperback edition
ISBN: 978-1-5458-0686-9 hardcover edition

www.papercutz.com

Papercutz books may be purchased for business or promotional use. For information on bulk purchases please contact Macmillan Corporate and Premium Sales Department at (800) 221-7945 x5442.

Printed in Turkey
October 2020

Distributed by Macmillan
First Printing

MEET THE LOUD FAMILY *and friends!*

LINCOLN LOUD
THE MIDDLE CHILD (11)

At 11 years old, Lincoln is the middle child, with five older sisters and five younger sisters. He has learned that surviving the Loud household means staying a step ahead. He's the man with a plan, always coming up with a way to get what he wants or deal with a problem, even if things inevitably go wrong. Being the only boy comes with some perks. Lincoln gets his own room – even if it's just a converted linen closet. On the other hand, being the only boy also means he sometimes gets a little too much attention from his sisters. They mother him, tease him, and use him as the occasional lab rat or fashion show participant. Lincoln's sisters may drive him crazy, but he loves them and is always willing to help out if they need him.

LORI LOUD
THE OLDEST (17)

As the first-born child of the Loud Clan, Lori sees herself as the boss of all her siblings. She feels she's paved the way for them and deserves extra respect. Her signature traits are rolling her eyes, texting her boyfriend, Bobby, and literally saying "literally" all the time. Because she's the oldest and most experienced sibling, Lori can be a great ally, so it pays to stay on her good side, especially since she can drive.

LENI LOUD
THE FASHIONISTA (16)

Leni spends most of her time designing outfits and accessorizing. She always falls for Luan's pranks, and sometimes walks into walls when she's talking (she's not great at doing two things at once). Leni might be flighty, but she's the sweetest of the Loud siblings and truly has a heart of gold (even though she's pretty sure it's a heart of blood).

LUNA LOUD
THE ROCK STAR (15)

Luna is loud, boisterous and freewheeling, and her energy is always cranked to 11. She thinks about music so much that she even talks in song lyrics. On the off-chance she doesn't have her guitar with her, everything can and will be turned into a musical instrument. You can always count on Luna to help out, and she'll do most anything you ask, as long as you're okay with her supplying a rocking guitar accompaniment.

LUAN LOUD
THE JOKESTER (14)

Luan's a standup comedienne who provides a nonstop barrage of silly puns. She's big on prop comedy too – squirting flowers and whoopee cushions – so you have to be on your toes whenever she's around. She loves to pull pranks and is a really good ventriloquist – she is often found doing bits with her dummy, Mr. Coconuts. Luan never lets anything get her down; to her, laughter IS the best medicine.

MR COCONUTS

Luan Loud's wise-cracking dummy.

LYNN LOUD
THE ATHLETE (13)

Lynn is athletic and full of energy and is always looking for a teammate. With her, it's all sports all the time. She'll turn anything into a sport. Putting away eggs? Jump shot! Score! Cleaning up the eggs? Slap shot! Score! Lynn is very competitive, but despite her competitive nature, she always tries to just have a good time.

BITEY

FANGS

LUCY LOUD
THE EMO (8)

You can always count on Lucy to give the morbid point of view in any given situation. She is obsessed with all things spooky and dark – funerals, vampires, séances, and the like. She wears mostly black and writes moody poetry. She's usually quiet and keeps to herself. Lucy has a way of mysteriously appearing out of nowhere, and try as they might, her siblings never get used to this.

LOLA LOUD
THE BEAUTY QUEEN (6)

Lola could not be more different from her twin sister, Lana. She's a pageant powerhouse whose interests include glitter, photo shoots, and her own beautiful, beautiful face. But don't let her cute, gap-toothed smile fool you; underneath all the sugar and spice lurks a Machiavellian mastermind. Whatever Lola wants, Lola gets – or else. She's the eyes and ears of the household and never resists an opportunity to tattle on troublemakers. But if you stay on Lola's good side, you've got yourself a fierce ally – and a lifetime supply of free makeovers.

LANA LOUD
THE TOMBOY (6)

Lana is the rough-and-tumble sparkplug counterpart to her twin sister, Lola. She's all about reptiles, mud pies, and muffler repair. She's the resident Ms. Fix-it and is always ready to lend a hand – the dirtier the job, the better. Need your toilet unclogged? Snake fed? Back-zit popped? Lana's your gal. All she asks in return is a little A-B-C gum, or a handful of kibble (she often sneaks it from the dog bowl).

LISA LOUD
THE GENIUS (4)

Lisa is smarter than the rest of her siblings combined. She'll most likely be a rocket scientist, or a brain surgeon, or an evil genius who takes over the world. Lisa spends most of her time working in her lab (the family has gotten used to the explosions), and says her research leaves little time for frivolous human pursuits like "playing" or "getting haircuts." That said, she's always there to help with a homework question, or to explain why the sky is blue, or to point out the structural flaws in someone's pillow fort. Lisa says it's the least she can do for her favorite test subjects, er, siblings.

LILY LOUD
THE BABY (15 MONTHS)

Lily is a giggly, drooly, diaper-ditching free spirit, affectionately known as "the poop machine." You can't keep a nappy on this kid – she's like a teething Houdini. But even when Lily's running wild, dropping rancid diaper bombs, or drooling all over the remote, she always brings a smile to everyone's face (and a clothespin to their nose). Lily is everyone's favorite little buddy, and the whole family loves her unconditionally.

CHARLES

WALT

CLIFF

GEO

RITA LOUD

Mother to the eleven Loud kids, Mom (Rita Loud) wears many different hats. She's a chauffeur, homework-checker and barf-cleaner-upper all rolled into one. She's always there for her kids and ready to jump into action during a crisis, whether it's a fight between the twins or Leni's missing shoe. When she's not chasing the kids around or at her day job as a dental hygienist for Dr. Feinstein, Mom pursues her passion: writing. She also loves taking on house projects and is very handy with tools (guess that's where Lana gets it from). Between writing, working and being a mom, her days are always hectic but she wouldn't have it any other way.

LYNN LOUD SR.

Dad (Lynn Loud Sr.) is a fun-loving, upbeat aspiring chef. A kid-at-heart, he's not above taking part in the kids' zany schemes. In addition to cooking, Dad loves his van, playing the cowbell and making puns. Before meeting Mom, Dad spent a semester in England and has been obsessed with British culture ever since – and sometimes "accidentally" slips into a British accent. When Dad's not wrangling the kids, he's pursuing his dream of opening his own restaurant where he hopes to make his "Lynn-sagnas" world-famous.

CLYDE McBRIDE
THE BEST FRIEND

Clyde is Lincoln's partner in crime. He's always willing to go along with Lincoln's crazy schemes (even if he sees the flaws in them up-front). Lincoln and Clyde are two peas in a pod and share pretty much all of the same tastes in movies, comics, TV shows, toys—you name it. As an only child, Clyde envies Lincoln—how cool would it be to always have siblings around to talk to? But since Clyde spends so much time at the Loud household, he's almost an honorary sibling anyway.

CLEOPAWTRA
Clyde's Cat

NEPURRTITI
Clyde's Other Cat

RUSTY SPOKES

Rusty is a self-proclaimed ladies' man who's always the first to dish out girl advice—even though he's never been on an actual date. His dad owns a suit rental service, so occasionally Rusty can hook the gang up with some dapper duds—just as long as no one gets anything dirty.

ZACH GURDLE

Zach is a self-admitted nerd who's obsessed with aliens and conspiracy theories. He lives between a freeway and a circus, so the chaos of the Loud House doesn't faze him. He and Rusty occasionally butt heads, but deep down, it's all love.

LIAM

Liam is an enthusiastic, sweet-natured farm boy full of down-home wisdom. He loves hanging out with his Mee Maw, wrestling his prize pig Virginia, and sharing his farm-to-table produce with the rest of the gang.

STELLA

Stella, 11, is a quirky, carefree girl who's new to Royal Woods. She has tons of interests, like trying on wigs, playing laser tag, eating curly fries, and hanging with her friends. But what she loves the most is tech — she always wants to dismantle electronics and put them back together again.

RONNIE ANNE SANTIAGO

Ronnie Anne's an independent spirit who's into skating, gaming and pranking. Strong-willed and a little gruff, she isn't into excessive displays of emotion. But don't be fooled – she has a sweet side, too, fostered by years of taking care of her mother and brother. And though her new extended family can be a little overwhelming, she appreciates how loving, caring, and fun they can be.

BOBBY SANTIAGO

Ronnie Anne's older brother, Bobby is a sweet, responsible, loyal high-school senior who works in the family's bodega. Bobby is very devoted to his family. He's Grandpa's right hand man and can't wait to one day take over the bodega for him. Bobby's a big kid and a bit of a klutz, which sometimes gets him into pickles, like locking himself in the freezer case. But he makes up for any work mishaps with his great customer skills – everyone in the neighborhood loves him.

MARIA CASAGRANDE SANTIAGO

She's the mother of Bobby and Ronnie Anne. A hardworking nurse, she doesn't get to spend a lot of time with her kids, but when she does she treasures it. Maria is calm and rational but often worries about whether she's doing enough for her kids. Maria, Bobby, and Ronnie Anne are a close-knit trio who were used to having only each other – until they moved in with their extended family.

HECTOR CASAGRANDE

He's the father of Carlos and Maria and the grandfather of six. The patriarch of the Casagrande Family, Hector wears the pants in the family (or at least thinks he does). He is the owner of the bodega on the ground floor of their apartment building and takes great pride in his work, his family, and being the unofficial "mayor" of the block. He's charismatic, friendly, and also a huge gossip (although he tries to deny it).

ROSA CASAGRANDE

She's the mother of Carlos and Maria and wife to Hector. Rosa is a gifted cook and has a sixth sense about knowing when anyone in her house is hungry. The wisest of the bunch, Rosa is really the head of the household but lets Hector think he is. She's spiritual and often tries to fix problems or illnesses with home remedies or potions. She's protective of all her family and at times can be a bit smothering.

CARLOS CASAGRANDE

He's the father of four kids (Carlota, CJ, Carl, and Carlitos), husband of Frida, and brother of Maria. He's a professor of marine biology at a local college and always has his head in a book. He's a pretty easygoing guy compared to his sometimes overly emotional relatives. Carlos is pragmatic, a caring father, and loves to rattle off useless tidbits of information.

FRIDA PUGA CASAGRANDE

She's the mother to Carlota, CJ, Carl, and Carlitos and wife to Carlos. She's an artist-type, always taking photos of the family. She tends to cry when she's overcome with sadness, anger, happiness... basically, she cries a lot. She's excitable, game for fun, passionate, and loves her family more than anything. All she ever wants is for her entire family to be in the same room. But when that happens, all she can do is cry and take photos.

CARLOTA CASAGRANDE

The oldest child of Carlos and Frida. She's social, fun-loving, and desperately wants to be the big sister to Ronnie Anne. Carlota has a very distinctive vintage style, which she tries to share with Ronnie Anne, who couldn't be less interested.

CJ (CARLOS JR.) CASAGRANDE

CJ was born with Down syndrome. He's the sunshine in everyone's life and always wants to play. He will often lighten the mood of a tense situation with his honest remarks. He adores Bobby and always wants to be around him (which is A-OK with Bobby, who sees CJ as a little brother). CJ asks to wear a bowtie every day no matter the occasion and is hardly ever without a smile on his face. He's definitely a glass-half-full kind of guy.

CARL CASAGRANDE

Carlino is 6 going on 30. He thinks of himself as a suave, romantic ladies' man. He's confident and outgoing. When he sees something he likes, he goes for it (even if it's Bobby's girlfriend, Lori). He cares about his appearance even more than Carlota and often uses her hair products (much to her chagrin). He hates to be reminded that he's only six and is emasculated whenever someone notices him snuggling his blankie or sucking his thumb. Carl is convinced that Bobby is his biggest rival and is always trying to beat Bobby (which Bobby is unaware of).

CARLITOS CASAGRANDE

The redheaded toddler who is always mimicking everyone's behavior, even the dog's. He's playful, rambunctious, and loves to play with the family pets.

LALO

SERGIO

MRS. APPLEBLOSSOM

BENNY STEIN

Benny is Luan's classmate, costar, and boyfriend. He's shy and quirky, but also sweet and earnest. He's not a zany comedian like Luan, but he sure enjoys her sense of humor and appreciates her wicked skills when it comes to prop comedy. Luan keeps Benny laughing, and Benny keeps Luan from sweating the small stuff. And as his marionette, Mrs. Appleblossom, would remind him (in her sassy British accent), it's all small stuff.

SID CHANG

Sid is Ronnie Anne's quirky best friend. She's new to the city but dives head-first into everything she finds interesting. She and her family just moved into the apartment one floor above the Casagrandes. In fact, Sid's bedroom is right above Ronnie Anne's! A dream come true for any BFFs.

STANLEY CHANG

Stanley Chang is Sid's dad. He's a conductor on the GLART-train that runs through the city. He's a patient man who likes to do Tai Chi when he gets stressed out. He likes to cheer up train commuters with fun facts, but emotionally he breaks down more than the train does.

BECCA CHANG

Becca Chang is Sid's mom. Like her daughter, Becca is quirky, smart, and funny. She works at the Great Lakes City Zoo and often brings her work home with her, which means the Chang household can also be a bit of a zoo!

ADELAIDE CHANG

Adelaide Chang is Sid's little sister. She's 6 years old, and has a flair for the dramatic. You can always find her trying to make her way into her big sister Sid's adventures.

"HUNG WITH CARE"

OF COURSE, SHE CAN MAKE AN ORNAMENT! WE ALL MADE ONE AT HER AGE.
WE DID?
OF COURSE!
OH, MY GOSH...
THAT REMINDS ME...I WAS SAVING THIS *MINT* FOR LATER!
⇒SIGH⇐ I'LL SHOW YOU...
THIS IS *LINCOLN'S.*
?

WE WERE SO EXCITED TO FINALLY GET A BROTHER!
I'M STARTING TO REALIZE WHY I FORGOT ABOUT MAKING THIS...
PULL DOWN MORE!
THIS IS LOLA AND LANA'S ORNAMENT. ITS TWO SIDED SINCE THEY MADE IT TOGETHER.
TIARAS!
EVEN THEN SHE LIKED CROWNS!
WHAT DOES LANA'S SIDE LOOK LIKE?
LOLA
Flip
LOLA
GROSS! GAG!
WHAT ABOUT THESE?

OH, THAT'S LISA'S! SO PRETTY!
SHE MADE THAT WHEN SHE WAS ONE?
YOU MAKE IT SOUND LIKE IT'S DIFFICULT.
I BET LYNN AND LUAN MADE THESE!
OH! OH! I KNOW THIS ONE! THAT'S LUNA'S!
BUT THE OTHER ONE I'M NOT QUITE SURE...
THAT ONE'S MINE! SHE'S SO STYLISH!
ARE YOU TRYING TO FIND YOUR ORNAMENT?
I'M TRYING. BUT THESE AREN'T EXACTLY EASY TO REACH...
WHOA!
CLIFF! NO!

MREOW?
CRASH
WELL, THAT WAS UNEXPECTED.
LOOKS LIKE INSTEAD OF STRAW, THE CAT BROKE THE CAMEL'S BACK. HUH? HUH? TOO SOON?
WAIT! THERE'S A CAMEL?
TOO SOON, BRO...
CLIFF! CLIFF!
LOOKS LIKE CLIFF WAS THE ONE WHO HELPED HER THE MOST WITH HER ORNAMENT.
MEOW!
GIGGLE. GIGGLE.
END

"COCOA LOCO"

THANKS FOR THE EPIC SNOWBALL FIGHT, GUYS! SAME TIME TOMORROW!
THANKS FOR **NOT** HITTING ME IN THE FACE, **NIKKI!**
BRRR... THAT WAS GREAT BUT I AM **FREEZING!**
YOU SAID IT. I CAN'T FEEL MY SPLEEN.
YOU KNOW WHAT I COULD REALLY GO FOR?
YOON KWAN COOKING YOU YOON KWAN SHAPED WAFFLES?
EH, CLOSE. GUESS ON THREE!
1... 2... 3...
HOT CHOCOLATE!

COME ON, SID!
HUFF! HOT...
PUFF! CHOCOLATE...
WHEEZE! PLEASE!
OH, SID MUST HAVE TOLD YOU ABOUT MY FAMOUS CHINESE 5 SPICE HOT CHOCOLATE. CHOCA-CHOCA. WOO-WOO!
NO, I AM SURE RONNIE ANNE TOLD SID ABOUT MY TRADITIONAL MEXICAN HOT CHOCOLATE.
OH, REALLY, ROSA? CARE FOR A LITTLE FRIENDLY COMPETITION?
REALLY, NO NEED FOR THIS!
YEAH, AS LONG AS IT'S HOT AND CHOCOLATE, WE'RE GOOD
OH, IT'S ON LIKE FLAN, STANLEY CHANG!

THE SECRET TO MY RECIPE IS A CINNAMON STICK AND *PILONCILLO*. THAT'S SPECIAL MEXICAN SUGAR!
OOOO!
THE SECRET IS MILK CHOCOLATE AND A SPOONFUL OF MY HOMEMADE CHINESE FIVE SPICE MIX.
AH!
THIS MOLINILLO WAS MY GREAT-GRANDMOTHER'S. SPIN IT BETWEEN YOUR HANDS AND MIX IT ALL TOGETHER.
LIKE THIS?
SPLAF
WHOOSH
WHOOPSIES!
...AND TOP IT WITH A BIG MARSHMALLOW.
MR. CHANG, THIS SMELLS AMAZING!
WELL, THEY DON'T CALL ME "HOT CHOCOLATE CHANG" FOR NOTHING!
WHO CALLS YOU THAT?

OKAY, ABUELA, YOU DRINK MR. CHANG'S. MR. CHANG, DRINK ABUELA'S.
FINALLY! I'M GOING TO DRINK EVERYTHING!
SLLLUUUURRRP
WOW!
ROSA, THESE FLAVORS! AND THE CREAMINESS! IT'S SO FROTHY!
OOO! IT'S GOT A KICK. I LOVE IT!
SID, DON'T TELL ABUELA BUT I THINK I HAVE A NEW FAVORITE.
THIS IS LIKE A HOT CHOCOLATE DANCE PARTY IN MY MOUTH!
WELL, GIRLS...?
HMM, I DON'T KNOW IF I CAN CHOOSE. THEY'RE BOTH SOOO GOOD!
HOW ABOUT A REMATCH? SAME TIME TOMORROW!

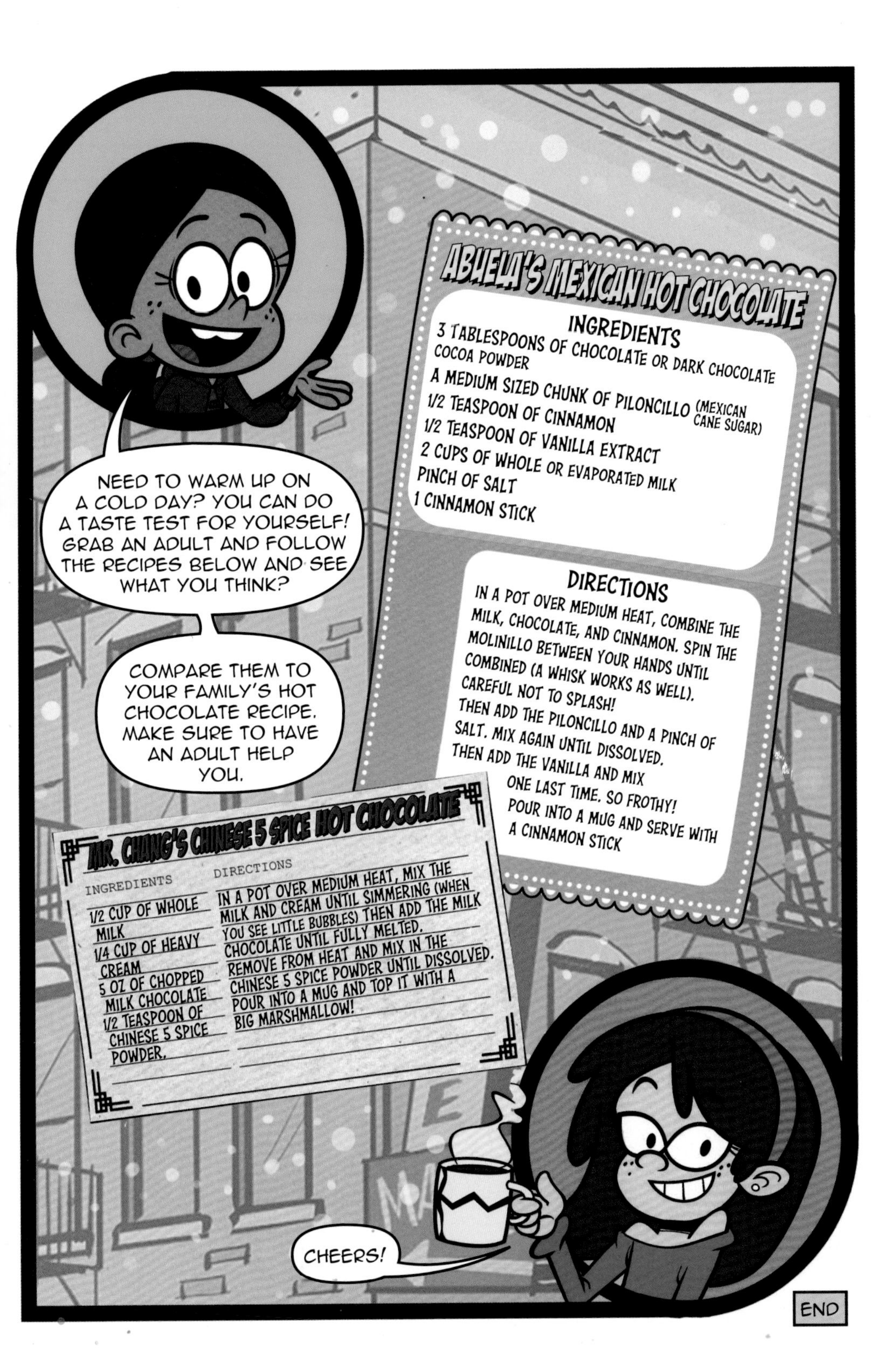
NEED TO WARM UP ON A COLD DAY? YOU CAN DO A TASTE TEST FOR YOURSELF! GRAB AN ADULT AND FOLLOW THE RECIPES BELOW AND SEE WHAT YOU THINK?
COMPARE THEM TO YOUR FAMILY'S HOT CHOCOLATE RECIPE. MAKE SURE TO HAVE AN ADULT HELP YOU.
ABUELA'S MEXICAN HOT CHOCOLATE
INGREDIENTS
3 TABLESPOONS OF CHOCOLATE OR DARK CHOCOLATE COCOA POWDER
A MEDIUM SIZED CHUNK OF PILONCILLO (MEXICAN CANE SUGAR)
1/2 TEASPOON OF CINNAMON
1/2 TEASPOON OF VANILLA EXTRACT
2 CUPS OF WHOLE OR EVAPORATED MILK
PINCH OF SALT
1 CINNAMON STICK
DIRECTIONS
IN A POT OVER MEDIUM HEAT, COMBINE THE MILK, CHOCOLATE, AND CINNAMON. SPIN THE MOLINILLO BETWEEN YOUR HANDS UNTIL COMBINED (A WHISK WORKS AS WELL). CAREFUL NOT TO SPLASH!
THEN ADD THE PILONCILLO AND A PINCH OF SALT. MIX AGAIN UNTIL DISSOLVED.
THEN ADD THE VANILLA AND MIX ONE LAST TIME. SO FROTHY!
POUR INTO A MUG AND SERVE WITH A CINNAMON STICK
MR. CHANG'S CHINESE 5 SPICE HOT CHOCOLATE
INGREDIENTS
1/2 CUP OF WHOLE MILK
1/4 CUP OF HEAVY CREAM
5 OZ OF CHOPPED MILK CHOCOLATE
1/2 TEASPOON OF CHINESE 5 SPICE POWDER.
DIRECTIONS
IN A POT OVER MEDIUM HEAT, MIX THE MILK AND CREAM UNTIL SIMMERING (WHEN YOU SEE LITTLE BUBBLES) THEN ADD THE MILK CHOCOLATE UNTIL FULLY MELTED.
REMOVE FROM HEAT AND MIX IN THE CHINESE 5 SPICE POWDER UNTIL DISSOLVED.
POUR INTO A MUG AND TOP IT WITH A BIG MARSHMALLOW!
CHEERS!
END

“PUPPET PUNISHMENT”

HUH? HUH? GET IT?

A-PIERS! LIKE "APPEARS", BUT WITH THE WORD "PIER"!

GROAN!
SLAP
HAHAHAHA!
GROAN!
SLAP

IF THERE'S ONE THING WE CAN AGREE ON...

DAD'S JOKES ARE ALL WASHED UP!
HEY!
END

"SLEDDIN' THE GNAR"

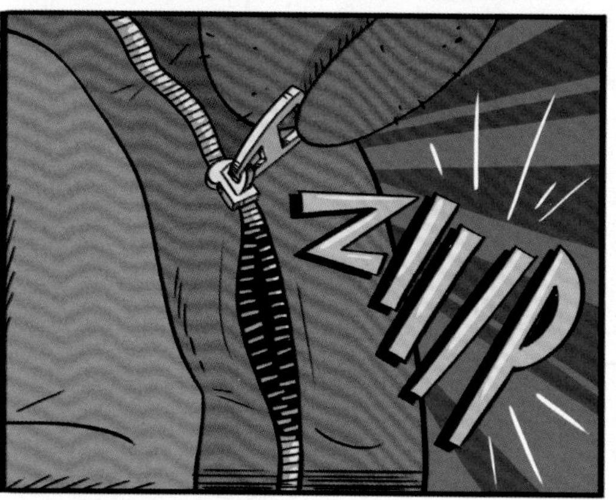

ENJOY YOUR GAME OF CARDS, I GUESS.
OKAY! HAVE A GOOD TIME SLIDING DOWN A HILL OF ICE AT HIGH SPEEDS!

ZIP

POP

GASP!

RONNIE ANNE! HELP!
OH, NO!

HE'S HEADING TO THE TOP OF THE SLEDDING HILL!

HEY!
NO CUTTING!
MEH. IT WOULDN'T BE THE FIRST TIME.

EEEH?
UH... SURE, I GUESS.

YEAH! GO, LITTLE DUDE!

SID, WE HAVE TO GO AFTER HIM!
UH, YOU GO, RONNIE ANNE. I DON'T REALLY NEED TO GO DO--

OOOWM!

WOO-HOO!

AH, YEAH!
AH, **NO!**

SWOOSH

SWOOSH
USH!

WOOOOOOOOOO!
I CAN'T LOOK!

MAKE IT STOP!

SWEET JUMPS, MY MAN!
YOU'RE MY HERO!
THAT WAS AMAZING!
PHEW! WE MADE IT!

NOW THAT WAS THE CRAZIEST THING YOU'VE EVER DONE!
THANK YOU.

HEY... WAIT A MINUTE! HOW DID YOU ALL GET DOWN HERE SO FAST, NIKKI?
OH, WE TOOK THE EASY ROUTE.

THERE'S AN EASY ROUTE?!
OH, SID!
HA
HA
HA
HA
HA
HA
HA
HA
HA
HA
HA
THE END

"I, Lily"

ISN'T IT FUN TO WATCH YOUR SISTER'S FIGURE-SKATING LESSON, *LILY?*
HMMPH. WIWWY WANT TV!
OKAY, LOUD. LET'S SEE THAT BUNNY HOP!

HUH?

GASP!
CLAP CLAP CLAP

WIWWY WANT SKATE! WIWWY WANT SKATE!
WELL, THAT WAS A QUICK TURN.

BUT YOU'RE THE RIGHT AGE FOR *NAPPING*, SWEETIE, NOT FOR SKATING.
YAWN!

YAWN. WIWWY SKATE--

SKATE, ALREADY!
WAH?
HURRY UP! I'M FREEZING MY TIARA OFF!
GASP!
YAY! GO, LILY! WE LOVE YOU!
WHEE!
COO!
PBBFT
HEE!
HEE!
HEE!
UGH, OF COURSE...
TEE-HEE!

FIGURE EIGHT? MORE LIKE FIGURE TEN OUT OF TEN!
10
10
CLAP
CLAP
CLAP

THAT... WAS... INCREDIBLE! SNIFF!
CLAP
CLAP
CLAP

CONGRATS! YOU WON THE GOLD MEDAL AT THE BABY OLYMPICS!
GASP!

LILY! LILY! LILY!

I WONDER WHAT SHE'S DREAMING ABOUT?
I DON'T KNOW BUT WAKE HER UP! I'M FREEZING MY TIARA OFF!
END

"BEST IN SNOW"

PLOSH PLOSH PLOSH
CLOP
PLOOP
PLOSH PLOSH PLOSH
.....
FLAP FLAP
CHARLES! SNOW IS ONLY FUN OUTSIDE!
THE END

"GEO'S NEW HOME"

CONTINUING ON, HE FOLLOWS A SCENT...
BURP!
AND COMES UPON A CRAZY TENT!
WITH UNFORTUNATE LUCK, GEO STEPS DOWN...
TWANG
SPLAT
AND BECOMES THE VICTIM OF A SUGARY CLOWN.
LOOKS LIKE YOU JUST GOT *CREAMED!*
WITH A FACE FULL OF CREAM, GEO GOES ON...

AND FINDS HIMSELF ON STAGE DURING A ROCKING SONG...
THE LIGHTS ARE BLARING, THE CROWD GOES WILD...
CLICK
AS GEO BLASTS OFF IN STYLE...
WAY TO *BLAST IT*, LI'L DUDE!
HE FINDS HIMSELF IN A MYSTERIOUS PLACE...
PLOP
WHERE GUMBALLS BOUNCE RIGHT AT HIS FACE...
BOING
BOING
BOING
WITH GRACE AND SPEED, HE DODGES THE THREAT...
BOING
BOING
BOING
WAK
AND SHOOTS A GOAL RIGHT INTO THE NET!
SWOOSH
GOOOOOOOALLL!

AS THE NIGHT WEARS ON, GEO ARRIVES...
AT THE LAIR WHERE A SUPER-SAVVY HERO RESIDES!
DARK AND MYSTERIOUS, WITH A MASK SO COOL...
CRACK
ALAS, HE FALLS TO A FATE SO CRUEL...
DANG IT!
TWO HOUSES NOW STAND IN HIS WAY. IN WHICH WILL HE CHOOSE TO STAY?
THE HOUSE OF GROSS RUBBISH, WITH SMELLS GALORE?
OR THE HOUSE OF PINK SPARKLES AND FANCY DECOR?

NEITHER, FOR HE HAS OTHER PLACES TO SEE....
LIKE A LAB OF STRANGE GOO AND MONSTER CANDY...
I'VE BEEN WAITING FOR YOUR ARRIVAL!
LISA, GEO IS NOT YOUR GUINEA PIG!
I THOUGHT HE WAS A HAMSTER?
GEO KNEW THIS WAS NOT RIGHT...
COFF. COFF.
FOR THE MOST EPIC OF HOUSES WAS FINALLY IN SIGHT!
AHEM.
HE ENTERS AND MARVELS AT THE GOTHIC DISPLAY.
AND WONDERS WHAT TREASURES ARE HIDDEN AWAY?
SURPRISE! EDWIN HAS RISEN AGAIN....
WILL GEO STAY? LET THE BATTLE BEGIN!

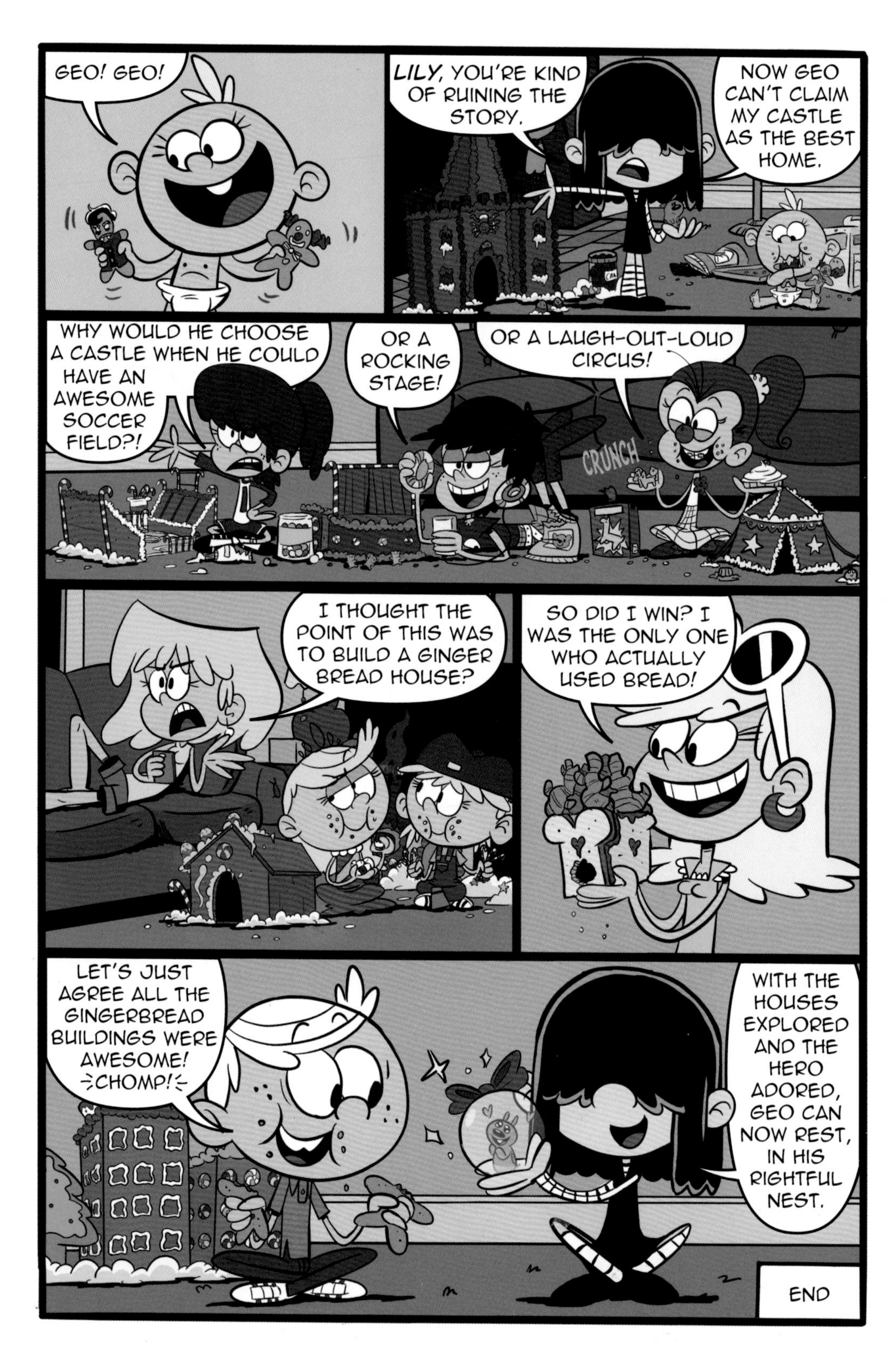
GEO! GEO!
LILY, YOU'RE KIND OF RUINING THE STORY.
NOW GEO CAN'T CLAIM MY CASTLE AS THE BEST HOME.
WHY WOULD HE CHOOSE A CASTLE WHEN HE COULD HAVE AN AWESOME SOCCER FIELD?!
OR A ROCKING STAGE!
OR A LAUGH-OUT-LOUD CIRCUS!
CRUNCH
I THOUGHT THE POINT OF THIS WAS TO BUILD A GINGER BREAD HOUSE?
SO DID I WIN? I WAS THE ONLY ONE WHO ACTUALLY USED BREAD!
LET'S JUST AGREE ALL THE GINGERBREAD BUILDINGS WERE AWESOME! CHOMP!
WITH THE HOUSES EXPLORED AND THE HERO ADORED, GEO CAN NOW REST, IN HIS RIGHTFUL NEST.
END

"BARNYARD BLIZZARD"

ZZZZ

PAT
PAT

WHOOOSH
...

ZZZZ
ZZZZ
THE END

"A GLITTERING RECIPE"

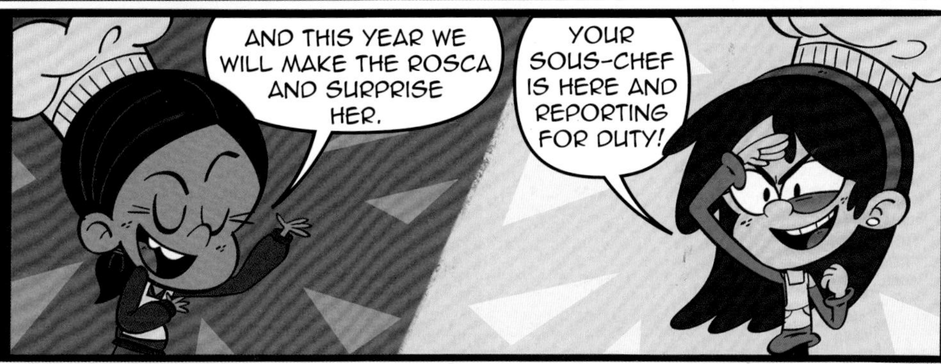

I WAS! BUT I'M ALL DONE WITH FROGGY 2'S GLO UP. LOOK, I EVEN USED MY SPECIAL GLITTER SPRAY.

SORRY, BUT ONLY CHEFS ALLOWED IN THE KITCHEN.

OKAY, SID, LET'S GET STARTED!
SLAP

4 HOURS LATER...
ZZZ
ZZZ

THE BREAD SHOULD BE DONE! I'LL CALL BOBBY!
DING

DON'T TRY THIS AT HOME. ALWAYS HAVE AN ADULT PRESENT TO HELP BAKE ANYTHING.

WHAT WILL WE DO?! ABUELA WILL BE HERE ANY--

HOLA MIJAS-- OH MI! THE KITCHEN?! WHAT HAPPENED?!

WE WANTED TO SURPRISE YOU BY MAKING ROSCA BUT--

BUT I RUINED IT. I'M SORRY, RONNIE ANNE!
SNIFF
SNIFF

...ITS OKAY, ADELAIDE. I KNOW YOU ONLY WANTED TO HELP.
I THINK I HAVE AN IDEA, MIJAS. TIE THOSE APRONS!

WOW, **MRS. CASAGRANDE!** THIS IS DELICIOUS! THANKS FOR SHOWING US HOW TO MAKE ROSCA.
YEAH, THANKS, ABUELA!
WELL, YOU ARE ALL GREAT SOUS-CHEFS!

ADELAIDE, THIS IS FOR YOU.

WOW! REALLY?!
YEAH! YOU'RE GOING TO NEED IT WHEN WE BAKE AGAIN.
RIBBIT!

NO MORE BAKING UNTIL MY KITCHEN GLITTERS IN THE LIGHT.
PLEASE, ABUELA, NO MORE GLITTER FOR AWHILE...
HAHAHAHA!
END

“FREEZE DAY”

AWWWW, MANNN...
WHAT'S UP, BUDDY?
I THINK MY LAPTOP'S BUSTED. IT'S COMPLETELY FROZEN!
WORLD
GEO

YOU KNOW COMPUTER STUFF, RIGHT *CLYDE?* CAN YOU HELP?
SORRY, PAL, NO CAN DO! MY TRICHOLOGIST WARNED ME BROKEN ELECTRONICS MIGHT AFFECT MY HAIR GROWTH.

DON'T WORRY, FELLAS!
THIS HAPPENS ALL THE TIME BACK HOME. WELL, KIND OF. JUST WITH GOATS!
GOATS...?

THAT'S RIGHT! OUR GOATS GET STUBBORN, AND WON'T MOVE!
IT'S LIKE THEY ARE FROZEN!
BUT I GOT A TRICK FOR THAT.

SOMETIMES, ALL A STUBBORN GOAT WANTS IS A GOOD HEADBUTT!

LIAM!
WHAT ARE YOU DOING?!

THAT'S NO WAY TO TREAT A COMPUTER!
OOF!!

THIS ISN'T A GOAT, IT'S A SLEEK, POWERFUL MACHINE!
YOU JUST GOTTA SWEET TALK IT A LIL'!

HEY THERE, BABY, I KNOW YOU'RE STRUGGLING. BUT, YOU KNOW, YOU'RE BEAUTIFUL, AND STRONG. I KNOW YOU CAN COME ROUND, YOU SWEET LITTLE--

EW, RUSTY, QUIT IT!
YOU DON'T NEED TO MARRY IT. THERE'S CLEARLY BEEN SOME ALIEN INTERFERENCE!

A LITTLE BLAST FROM THIS SUPER MAGNET SHOULD INTERRUPT THE FREQUENCY...
ZACH, NO!

THERE'S A CHANCE YOUR MAGNET COULD DAMAGE THE HARD DRIVE!

LINCOLN, HAVE YOU TRIED TURNING IT OFF AND ON AGAIN?

OH, LET ME TRY THAT NOW.

POWERING ON!
CLICK

YAY FOR STELLA!
THAT KITTY'S PURRING NOW!
YOU FIXED IT!

SIGH.
THE END

"MITTEN MAYHEM"

READY-TO-ROCK OR READY-FOR-THE GRAVE, THESE ARE STAR-STUDDED MITTENS FOR SURE!

WHOA! IT LOOKS LIKE THESE TWO ARE READY TO TAME A BULL WITH THOSE FIERY COLORS!

AND WHAT CAN WE SAY EXCEPT...
AAAAWWWWW!
HEY, KIDS...

YOU ALL KNOW I KEEP MORE GLOVES AND MITTENS IN THIS BAG, RIGHT? YOU CAN FIND ALL YOUR MATCHES HERE!

I DUNNO, I LIKE HOW WE LOOKED!
YEAH, LENI, GREAT JOB WITH THESE PAIRINGS!

MINE ARE SO FAB!
YEAH, MINE ROCK!
THANKS, LENI!

AW, I COULDN'T HAVE MORE **FASHIONABLE** SIBLINGS!
THE END

"MEOWY CATMAS"

HEH, HEH, HEH...
GROWL! ARF! YIP?
NICE TRY
MEOW?
HISS!
SPRITZ
PLOP
HMMM...
C&N
CLEOPAWTRA! NEPURRTITI!
C&N
SORRY, DADS. I GUESS MY PRECAUTIONS DIDN'T WORK.
THAT'S OKAY. IT LOOKS LIKE THEY WERE ONLY ABLE TO GET TO THEIR PRESENT FROM NANA GAYLE.
OOH! YOU KNOW WHAT THAT MEANS...
Happy Holidays from the McBrides!
END

"OPERATION: X-MAS"

ROGER, THIS IS LOLA. OPERATION "X-MAS" IS A GO.

WHO'S ROGER?
LEAVE IT TO ME, SIS. I LIKE GETTING MY HANDS DIRTY. THE EAGLE HAS LANDED AT LIAM'S.

WHAT EAGLE? I DON'T SEE ONE.
LENI, GET OFF THE LINE. SIGH.

FRET NOT, LANA. NOW, THIS PLAN IS FAIRLY DETAILED, SO TAKE NOTE.

PHASE 1 IS THE DROP OFF. DIRECT DELIVERY TO OUR CUSTOMER BASE DISGUISED AS PLAYDATES.
YOU CAN GO NOW, LENI.
GO WHERE? OH, OKAY... BYE!

IN PHASE 2, YOU'RE GOING TO USE MY INVENTION TO SEE THROUGH PRESENTS. REPORT BACK YOUR FINDINGS, OF COURSE.

BOY HOWDY!
GAME

IN PHASE 3, WE COLLECT OUR PAYMENT THROUGH ALLOWANCES.
PLEASURE DOING BUSINESS, ROXANNE.

PHASE 4. WAIT FOR EXTRACTION.
SQUAWK! SQUAWK! LOLA SAYS I AM THE EAGLE!

LOOKS LIKE "OPERATION: X-MAS" WAS A COMPLETE SUCCES--
SQUAWK!

GIRLS!
OH.

WELL, THANKS TO YOUR LITTLE "OPERATION" I GOT A CALL FROM LIAM'S MOTHER. SOMEHOW, HE FOUND OUT WHAT HE'S GETTING FOR CHRISTMAS EARLY.

BUT, FATHER, WHAT IF I WERE TO TELL YOU THAT CHRISTMAS COULD COME EARLY THIS YEAR?
HAVEN'T YOU WONDERED WHAT YOUR BIG TICKET PRESENT IS?

WOULD I?!

AHEM.

YOU'RE ALL GROUNDED!
CAN I GO BACK TO BEING LENI? MY WINGS ARE TIRED. NOW I KNOW HOW WALT FEELS.
END

UNLIKELY SUPERHEROES
YOU'RE NOT GOING TO GET AWAY WITH THE MARBLE STATUE!
OH, I ALREADY HAVE!
THAT'S WHAT YOU THINK! FANGS!
SWOOP
BOO!
ACK!
WHOSH

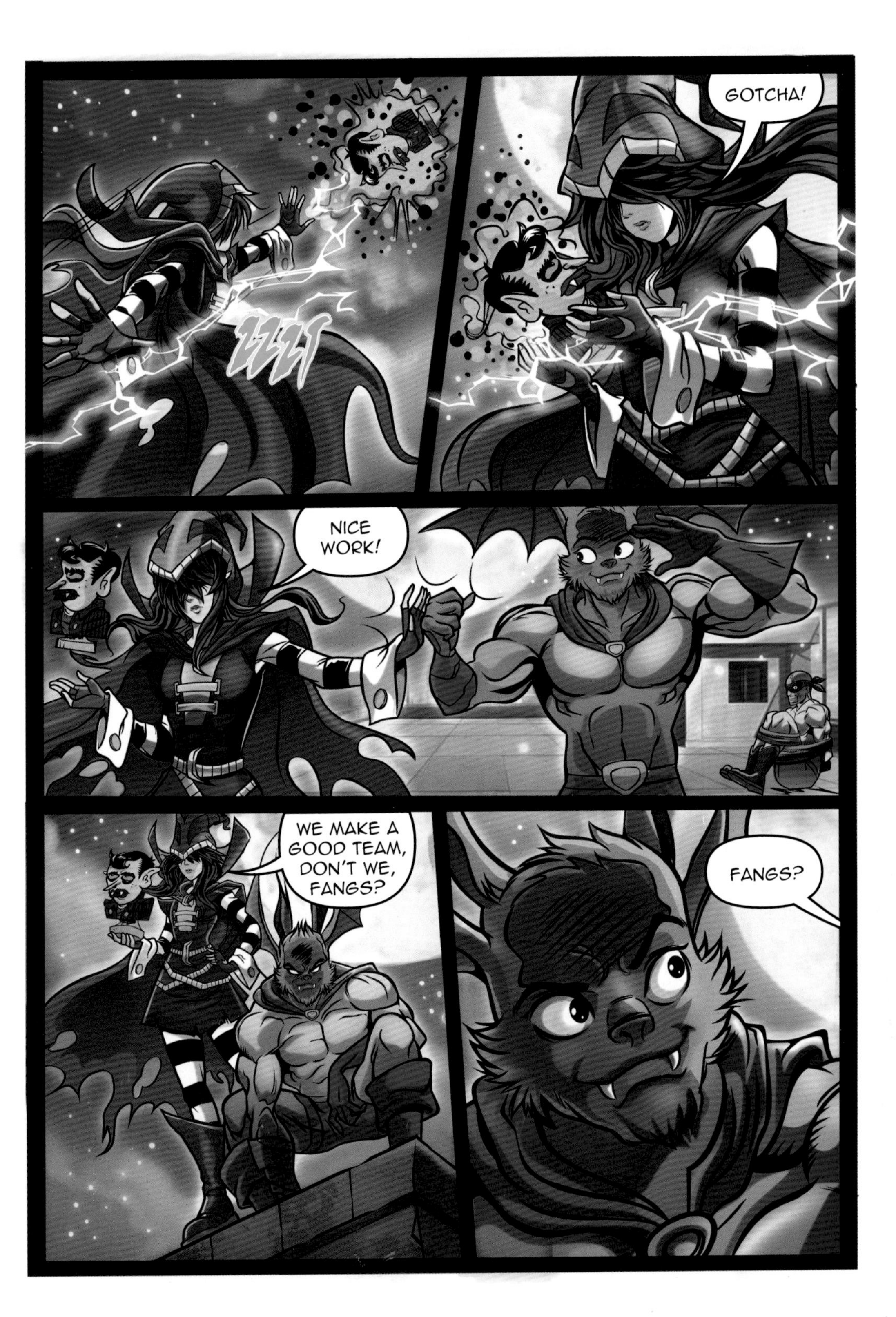
ZZZT
GOTCHA!
NICE WORK!
WE MAKE A GOOD TEAM, DON'T WE, FANGS?
FANGS?

FANGS!
YOU MUST BE TIRED...YOU FELL ASLEEP OFF OF YOUR PERCH, MY LITTLE CREATURE OF DARKNESS.
IT'S CHRISTMAS EVE... DID YOU WISH FOR ANYTHING?
WELL, I'M SORRY YOU'LL HAVE TO SLEEP THROUGH CHRISTMAS EVE...
...BUT I'LL BE SURE TO GIVE YOU A GIFT, SOON.
THE END

WATCH OUT FOR PAPERCUTZ™

We warmly welcome you to the frosty, fun-filled, first THE LOUD HOUSE WINTER SPECIAL graphic novel from Papercutz, those non-freezing folks dedicated to publishing great graphic novels for all ages. I'm Jim Salicrup, the Editor-in-Chief huddled up next to editor Jeff Whitman's personal space heater, here to tell you exactly what's so special about this WINTER SPECIAL and to mention another Papercutz series I'm sure you'll enjoy.

Since Papercutz started publishing THE LOUD HOUSE graphic novels there's been only one complaint—that there simply wasn't enough of them! True Loud House fans were bombarding us with emails, tweets, private messages, phone calls, and letters demanding that we publish more THE LOUD HOUSE graphic novels. We at Papercutz were eager to do so but it's not always that easy. Many of the writers and artists who create the comics for THE LOUD HOUSE graphic novels also work on the actual The Loud House show for Nickelodeon. In other words, they squeeze in writing and drawing THE LOUD HOUSE comics in their spare time, of which they increasingly don't have much. The solution was to find comics creators who also happen to be big fans of The Loud House, and have them write and draw more stories for THE LOUD HOUSE graphic novels! As a result, you've now got THE LOUD HOUSE WINTER SPECIAL, in addition to our regular ongoing THE LOUD HOUSE graphic novel series to meet the never-ending demand. But I suspect, fans may still want more…

And what I may try to do is convince them to try another new Papercutz series featuring a series that's almost the opposite of THE LOUD HOUSE. It's a series set long, long ago and takes place in a tiny village. While they're not necessarily all related, they are all taken care of by someone they call Papa. And while Lincoln Loud deals with living in the same house as his ten sisters, the one lone female in this village contends with about a hundred guys… each one as unique as each of Lincoln's sisters. If you're a Papercutz fan, then you've probably guessed I'm talking about THE SMURFS! Sure, they're each only three apples tall, but they're packed with personality! If you enjoy Leni Loud's fashion passion, you'll laugh at Vanity Smurf's antics. Or if you admire the athletic ambitions of Lynn Loud, you'll be impressed by Hefty Smurf's physical prowess. I'm sure if you laugh at Luan Loud's stand-up comedy, you'll get a blast out of Jokey Smurf's… shall we say, special gift? If you're impressed by the genius of Lisa Loud, Brainy Smurf will definitely amuse you. I could go on and on, but I think you're getting the idea. The new series is called THE SMURF TALES, and it'll be coming your way soon, but in the meantime you can catch up on their classic adventures in SMURFS 3 IN 1, which collects three great SMURFS graphic novels in one. Just like THE LOUD HOUSE 3 IN 1 graphic novels, in fact.

But we saved the best news for last; THE SMURFS will be appearing on the same channel as THE LOUD HOUSE in 2021! That's right, THE SMURFS are coming to Nickelodeon as a brand-new original series! You'll see the cartoons on Nickelodeon and enjoy the graphic novels from Papercutz. Isn't that just Smurftastic?

Thanks,

STAY IN TOUCH!

EMAIL:	salicrup@papercutz.com
WEB:	papercutz.com
TWITTER:	@papercutzgn
INSTAGRAM:	@papercutzgn
FACEBOOK:	PAPERCUTZGRAPHICNOVELS
FANMAIL:	Papercutz, 160 Broadway, Suite 700, East Wing, New York, NY 10038

Warm up with a special preview of THE LOUD HOUSE #11 "Who's the Loudest?"

"OCEAN 11"

IT LOOKS LIKE THERE'S SOMETHING INSIDE. A MESSAGE IN A BOTTLE.

PROBABLY THE ILL-FATED LAST WORDS FROM A SINKING SHIP.
THAT'S TOO DEPRESSING. I HOPE IT'S A ROMANTIC LETTER TO A LOVED ONE.

LET'S BREAK IT OPEN AND SEE!
NO! IT'S TOO BEAUTIFUL TO DESTROY.
IF IT'S OLD, THE EXPOSURE TO AIR MIGHT DISSOLVE THE PAPER. THIS REQUIRES A MORE SCIENTIFIC SOLUTION.

ALLOW ME...
TAP
POP

ANY GOOD JOKES WRITTEN ON IT? I'LL EVEN TAKE BAD ONES.
NO, ***LUAN!*** IT'S A TREASURE MAP!

ACCORDING TO THIS MAP, IT LOOKS LIKE THERE ARE CLUES SCATTERED AROUND THE BEACH THAT WILL LEAD US TO THE BURIED TREASURE.
LET'S DO THIS!

I'M ALREADY ON IT!

I FOUND THE TREASURE!
EWWWW.... GROSS!

NO, THANKS. I'LL LOOK FOR LOST LOVE ELSEWHERE.

LET ME SEE THAT MAP!
HEY!
THE KIDS APPEAR TO BE HAVING FUN.

AND IT ONLY TOOK ME A FEW MINUTES TO DRAW UP THAT MAP YESTERDAY.
YOU REALLY DID PACK EVERYTHING.
END